"Custard the Squirrel,
don't you think Custard the Squirrel
is a silly name?"

To Sophie and the real
Custard the Squirrel

The illustrations for this book were made with pen and ink and watercolor.

Cataloging-in-Publication Data has been applied for and may
be obtained from the Library of Congress.

ISBN 978-1-4197-5524-8

Text and illustrations © 2022 Sergio Ruzzier
Book design by Heather Kelly

Printed and bound in China
10 9 8 7 6 5 4 3 2 1

For bulk discount inquiries, contact specialsales@abramsbooks.com.

ABRAMS The Art of Books
195 Broadway, New York, NY 10007
abramsbooks.com

NO!
said Custard the Squirrel

SERGIO RUZZIER

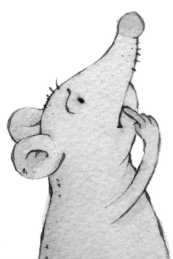

Abrams Appleseed
New York

"Custard the Squirrel,
aren't you a duck?"

"No," said Custard the Squirrel.

"Custard the Squirrel,
won't you go
swim in the lake?"

"No," said Custard the Squirrel.

"Custard the Squirrel,
will you please quack?"

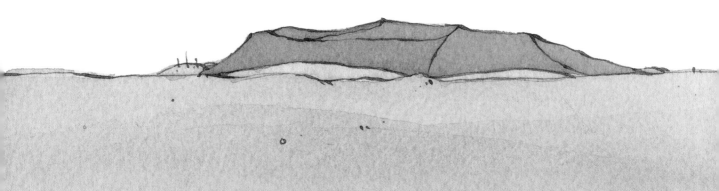

"No," said Custard the Squirrel.

"Custard the Squirrel,
eat some weeds!"

"No," said Custard the Squirrel.

"Custard the Squirrel,
can you please lay an egg?"

"No," said Custard the Squirrel.

"Custard the Squirrel . . ."

"No," said Custard the Squirrel.

"Custard the Squirrel,
do you only answer 'No'?"

"Yes!"

said Custard the Squirrel.